# Aloha-Ha! Adventures

*By*

*Roscoe Donaldson*

# Table of Contents

# Acknowledgements:

Co-Author - Debbie

Editor - Rebecca (rebeccarossediting@gmail.com)

Custom Artwork - Kristie

# Dedication

To our family and all our adventures!

# About the Author

Roscoe Donaldson has been writing his entire life. His first book, *Vacation of a Lifetime,* was published in 2023.

Roscoe lives on the Washington coast with his co-author Debbie. They have three adult children and one spoiled Siamese.

# Authors Notes

One of George and Martha Rainier's dream vacation destinations is Hawaii.

Warm winds with the scent of tropical flowers, amazing sunrises, swimming in the warm Pacific Ocean, and relaxing on the beach while watching the catamaran boats loaded with tourists sailing by on their way to enjoy a dinner cruise and watch the amazing sunset.

Hawaiian traditions such as making offerings called Ho'okupu to the island's gods and goddesses and honoring them and their spirituality.

The story you are about to read is based on real events. The names have been changed to protect the innocent and the potentially guilty.

This story is a retelling of our adventurous trip to Hawaii. Everything had been perfectly arranged. The purpose of this story is to remind everyone that nothing ever goes exactly as planned.

Always remember that sometimes you must go with the flow, bend with the wind, and dance in the rain.

Laugh because life is too short not to. Enjoy everything to the fullest, regardless of setbacks. Keep smiling and stay focused on the good things in life because that is what makes memories.

Thank you for taking the time to read this story.

# **Prologue**

Their day had not started off perfectly, but George and Martha were on vacation in Hawaii and determined to make the best out of everything.

They had their entire week's activities planned, including hiking, lots of beach time, and relaxing under the palm trees.

George and Martha had made a stop at a local deli to grab some sandwiches before spending the day at the beach. The temperatures were already in the 80s, and they were looking forward to lathering on coconut-scented sunscreen and enjoying the tropical breeze coming off the Pacific Ocean.

They parked the rental car, leaving their iced coffees in the cup holders, and locked the vehicle. They walked around the corner to the deli where they were going to get the sandwiches.

They pushed the door to the building open and were met with a frigid blast of air conditioning. They placed their orders and waited about ten minutes while the deli employees prepared their food. George paid the bill, and they began their walk back to the car.

George shuffled in his new flip-flops as they made their way back to the lot. He had found the flip-flops on sale right before their trip and regretted not taking the time to break them in. He hoped the pain he was feeling was not a blister beginning to form.

Everyone's arms were full of brown bags containing not only sandwiches but chips, sodas, bottled water, some chocolate for a treat, and lots of napkins! They rounded the corner to where they had left the car parked and glanced up just in time to see a tow truck speeding across the alley behind the lot with their rental car, including their iced coffees, attached to the towbar.

# Aloha-ha! Adventures!

There once was a couple named George and Martha who were obsessed with tropical vacations. Their obsession began when they spent their honeymoon in Hawaii. Even though they had previously been to the islands on family vacations while growing up separately, this was their first trip together as a married couple.

After spending a week on the big island of Hawaii and enjoying all the amenities of the island, they were hooked and tried to take vacations in warmer climates as much as possible.

George and Martha had been married for several years when they decided to expand their family. They were blessed with three children: Nadine, Colton, and Missy. Colton and Missy were twins and were born 20 months after their older sister, Nadine.

The year before the children graduated, Nadine from College and Colton and Missy from high school, George and Martha took them on a celebratory trip to Hawaii. They had hopes that their children would fall in love with tropical destinations as much as they had.

This graduation trip would be the first big family trip for them other than camping and "local" stays at hotels.

The family spent a week and a half on the Island of Oahu and had done nearly every touristy thing they could. They spent time at the beach and pool. They went to a luau, had an early morning tour of Pearl Harbor, an all-day island tour, and enjoyed a hula and magic show. This family vacation went off without a hitch and everyone came home tired, sunburned, and feeling that they needed a vacation to recover from their vacation.

Time went by, and the three Rainier children all went their separate ways. Nadine had taken a short sabbatical to California and made the decision that California was not for her and moved back home during the pandemic of 2020.

Colton had relocated to another state and obtained his engineering degree, and Missy had joined the workforce and relocated to another part of the state.

They all survived the pandemic of 2020 and the accompanying cabin fever. Everyone felt that they needed a vacation. Many ideas were discussed, and, of course, multiple tropical locations were considered.

Colton had been dating a young lady named Luna. Luna had lived in Hawaii her entire life. After Colton had graduated college, he and Nadine decided to travel to Hawaii to visit Luna and her family. They spent most of their time hiking, enjoying Hawaiian foods, and relaxing on the beach.

Now, Luna was preparing to graduate from college, and Colton said that he was planning to attend the graduation ceremony. Luna's plans were to relocate to Ohio with Colton after she graduated.

George, Martha, and Nadine decided that they wanted to travel to Hawaii to join Colton and meet Luna and her family. They made plans to attend her graduation ceremony and then enjoy a quiet, relaxing tropical vacation.

Everyone was able to book their tickets utilizing a "Black Friday" sale at the airlines. Colton would only have to switch planes three times to travel from Ohio to Honolulu. George, Martha, and Nadine would only have to change planes one time. The layover would be in

Maui for an hour. All things considered, not such a bad place to have a layover.

Missy decided to sit out this trip as she had a hectic work schedule and could not take the time off. The rest of the family was saddened by this and agreed that she would be missed.

It was a long winter as the four counted down the days until their vacation. During this time, Martha began doing research on places to stay and things to do within a reasonable distance of Luna's house and the graduation ceremony.

The group spent several days talking about different options for their trip, and it was decided that an Airbnb would be best. That way, they could cook meals, do laundry, and live in a house where they could come and go as they pleased, rather than a hotel or condominium where there were housekeepers that came in every day and people right next door that they didn't know. Eventually, they narrowed down the Airbnb selection to two choices and Luna was included in the conversation to help determine what area she thought was the best in which to stay.

The Airbnb was a four-bedroom, two-bath home situated on the backside of the Punchbowl crater. Glancing over the reviews, it seemed like it would be the perfect place, just a few miles from the stadium where the graduation would take place and about fifteen miles from Luna's house. Down payments were made, emails exchanged between the host and Martha, and soon they had a place to call their own while visiting the island.

Weekends that winter were spent talking on the phone, streaming movies together, and making plans. Luna had many activities she wanted them to experience and was excited that they would all finally get to meet face-to-face.

With most of the trip details complete, the weeks seemed to drag by as they anxiously awaited their vacation.

# **Monday**

George, Martha, and Nadine had planned to stay at a hotel near the airport the day before their flight. The car was loaded, the gas tank was full, and George and Martha were sitting in front of Nadine's office, waiting for her to get off work.

George and Martha had eaten a quick dinner and had picked up fast food for Nadine to eat on the way to the hotel.

Nadine finally completed her shift and came out the front door of the office, saying, "I'm on vacation!" She quickly dropped her backpack in the back of the car, climbed in the backseat, and fastened her seatbelt. Martha all but squealed the tires on the car as they left the parking lot on the way to the hotel!

Nadine finished her *a la carte* meal, and everyone was attempting to avoid the frustration with the traffic slow down by singing along with the radio. Suddenly, Nadine's phone rang. The radio was quickly turned off. "Hello? What's up?" asked Nadine.

Colton was on the other end of the call, saying that because of the thunderstorms they were experiencing in Ohio, his first flight had been canceled, and now he was scrambling to get on a flight that could similarly match the schedule that had been prepared so many months before. It took about thirty minutes, thirty long… stressful… minutes, to find a departing flight that could accommodate his traveling needs, and it only had one stop! The plane would depart Ohio at a later time and would land in Honolulu earlier than originally planned! Talk about a stroke of good luck!

Once Colton's new flights had been booked and confirmed, they determined that Luna would be the common connection regarding their travel details and updates. If they could not talk with each other, Luna would be the messenger for the others. The radio was turned back on, and their singing changed to songs of celebration for narrowly escaping what could have been a traveling disaster for Colton. The traffic had also thinned out, and they were back on schedule to arrive at the hotel.

The sun was setting, and it was beginning to get dark as they continued the drive to the Best Western, where they would be spending the night. Martha had booked a package where they were able to stay the night and leave the car at the hotel while they traveled. As they pulled into the covered driveway of the hotel, George unbuckled before the car came to a stop and went inside to check in at the front desk. George came back to the car with a parking pass in hand and directions to the long-term parking area, which was at the very edge of the main parking lot.

They found an adequate parking space, gathered all their belongings, and trudged across the dusty gravel parking lot and into the lobby. While they waited for the elevator that would whisk them all the way to the third floor, they played a game of rock, paper, and scissors to determine who would get first dibs on using the restroom after their long drive. Martha won the draw and all but ran down the hallway towards the room. Finally, they were all checked in at 10:00 pm and began counting down the time until they needed to be at the airport.

Once they were settled in their room, clothing for the next day of traveling was set aside, several alarms were set to ensure they would wake up on time, and luggage was gathered together to allow them to make a hasty exit in the morning.

With everything in place for the next day, they all collapsed in bed in anticipation of a restful night's sleep.

# Tuesday

George, Martha, and Nadine had a restless night's sleep. They tossed and turned and kept one eye open to keep watch of the time, worrying about the possibility of oversleeping and missing the airport shuttle. Finally, Martha looked at the clock and noticed it was only five minutes until the alarm would sound and decided to get an early start.

After their earlier-than-anticipated rising, they grabbed a quick breakfast consisting of sausage links and eggs in anticipation of a long day ahead. They loaded their baggage onto the shuttle that would take them to the airport. After all, they could sleep on the plane, or so they thought.

The shuttle driver must have been fresh off the Nascar racetrack. He sped from one hotel to another to pick up more passengers, ignoring speed limits and stop signs along the way. At one point they took a corner so quickly that people were almost tumbling out of their seats into the aisle. The three of them were thankful that their decision to get coffee had been delayed until arriving at the airport.

Upon arrival at the airport, nearly two and a half hours before their flight was scheduled to leave, the group checked in at the airline kiosk. There, it was discovered that although they had purchased these tickets months in advance, they would not be seated next to one another. George and Martha would sit together, and Nadine would be sitting with strangers.

Another stop was made at the baggage counter to check their suitcases which helped to lighten up their load. After checking their bags, they made two steps to the left and were immediately in line for TSA.

The TSA line moved very smoothly even though Martha and Nadine held up the line by nearly having to be strip searched. Not really, but they did have to be patted down, and their hands had to be swabbed because their wet hair, banded in clips caused them to be very suspicious.

In the meantime, George scrambled to the end of the conveyor belt and began grabbing everyone's belongings, all while clutching his pants around his waist to prevent an embarrassing scene as he had been required to remove his belt and feared that his palm tree boxers would be revealed to everyone in the airport.

Once they were all redressed, the next item on the agenda was the delayed coffee stop. Starbucks seemed to be a good option as it was located conveniently between the TSA checkpoint and the departure gates. Martha was left standing against the wall, guarding their luggage as Nadine and George stood in line for about ten minutes. They glanced at their phones and then at each other and thought, why were they standing in line when they could have used the mobile ordering app and saved those ten minutes of time?

Thank goodness Martha had woken up earlier than planned and that the shuttle driver had gotten them to the airport so quickly that they had the extra time to wait in line.

After they had obtained their liquid motivation, they decided a bathroom break was in order. All three of them could have been circus stars as they juggled their carry-on, a backpack, and now a hot cup of coffee while waiting to use the facilities. The ladies decided to pile up the carry-ons and backpacks, leaving charge of them with George while they took their turn in the restroom. They returned the favor of watching his belongings while George tended to business.

Finally arriving at the departure gate, the trio discovered there was no place for them all to sit. They decided to sit at the gate next to their assigned gate, within earshot, so they could listen for announcements about their flight. They passed the time reading, chatting, and drinking their coffee, all the while anxiously awaiting the plane that would whisk them away from the gray skies and damp weather they had been experiencing.

Fortunately, by the time the boarding announcements were made, the coffee cups had been drained and discarded, making their juggling act easier. The three stood in line for quite some time, waiting for the correct loading zone to be announced. Of course, they were in the very last zone to be boarded.

Excitement swelled as they finally set foot on the aircraft. The flight attendants directed George and Martha to go one way around a group of seats and Nadine to go the other. After a short, tearful goodbye, they found their assigned seats. The challenge continued because they had been the last to board; stowing their bags for the trip was not an easy task.

Settling into their seats, George and Martha looked across the plane and spotted Nadine sitting clear on the other side of the aircraft. Multiple waves were exchanged, and a mutual thumbs-up indicated that they were ready for takeoff.

The plane pulled away from the gate, and the atmosphere onboard was one of excitement and anticipation. Flight attendants gave their spiel about seatbelts, personal flotation devices, and overhead air masks while Hawaiian music played in the background. All the attendants were wearing blue flowered Hawaiian shirts and said "Aloha" and "Mahalo" multiple times to the passengers.

Everyone on board was excited to finally be beginning their adventures. Some were going on vacation, some were traveling for work, while others were returning home from their mainland visit.

As they patiently sat securely buckled in their seats, it felt like it took forever before the plane's engines fired up, and they began to move to the end of the runway. Once again, the aircraft came to a stop.

Suddenly, the overhead speaker growled to life as the pilot announced that the plane was now third in line to take off. The plane inched forward as the passengers watched other planes take off and land. Finally, the pilot maneuvered the aircraft in a half-circle at the end of the runway and lurched to a stop. Everything went silent. The overhead air that had been blowing so loudly, muffling the sounds of people's voices, stopped, causing all conversations to cease for the moment.

Ten seconds later, the engines revved back to life, and the aircraft jolted forward on the runway. The overhead air began flowing at a high rate again and the plane's nose tipped slightly upward as the ground began to move underneath the aircraft. Looking out of the windows, the buildings and grassy areas began to pass by at a faster rate. Almost magically, the rough movements from traveling down the runway stopped as the aircraft lifted off the ground and began to ascend into the cloudy skies above. A rough, rumbling mechanical noise could be heard as the landing gear was drawn into the belly of the plane. They were on their way!

**The Journey Begins!**

The airline provided a very nutritious meal if you were not diabetic like George or gluten intolerant like Martha. Martha wound up dissecting her sandwich in such a way that her eighth-grade biology teacher would have been impressed. Having surgically detached the lunch meat and cheese from her toasted sandwich, she managed to roll the remnants up into a delightful two-bite snack that had everyone onboard envious.

George choked down part of his carbohydrate-laced sandwich and then wound up extracting the meat and cheese as well. They had both opted for a soda to drink. The beverage had been served in flimsy plastic cups, and the rest of the can was left by the flight attendant to self-refill. After Martha had finished her lunch and swallowed down the last of her soda, she stacked her cup with Georges to make garbage disposal easier. She then threw her napkin into the top cup, which she did not realize was still one-third full of Georges' soda. The napkin managed to absorb most of what liquid was left so they opted to dispose of the trash at their earliest convenience.

After the very filling meal, the rest of the flight was spent either napping, watching an onboard movie, or playing video games on the television screens on the headrest of the seat directly in front of their assigned seats. A few hours later, the pilot's voice came over the loudspeaker, announcing their descent to Maui.

The flight coming into Maui was very turbulent. Martha and Nadine felt as if the meager meal they had enjoyed earlier might make a reappearance. Once the plane landed and taxied to the gate, they both quickly made their way to the restrooms. The warm tropical air and being back on the ground seemed to help settle their stomachs, and the meal stayed where it was supposed to.

To be on the safe side, they decided they would purchase a soda and a salty snack in an attempt to settle their still somewhat upset stomachs. The girls stayed with the luggage while George took his turn with the restroom. While in the restroom, George had taken his phone from his pocket so that he could check his email and laid it down on the TP dispenser. After washing his hands and exiting the restroom, he patted his pocket and realized his phone was still in the restroom stall he had used. He quickly backtracked and fortunately found his phone right where he had left it, all the while thinking, *I hope this is not a precursor to the rest of the trip!*

While waiting for their connecting flight to Oahu, the airline announced that their departure gate had been changed. They gathered their belongings and made their way through the airport to the new loading area and were awaiting further instructions when they noticed that there was no plane at the new gate. Apparently, the connecting plane had been delayed, which caused their departure to be delayed by 40 minutes.

Nadine's fingers flew over the keyboard of her phone as she kept Luna updated. Luna told Nadine that Colton would be arriving thirty minutes before them and would meet them in the Honolulu airport.

The flight from Maui to Oahu was short, and they were finally able to all sit together and enjoy the turbulent takeoff and landing. Once again, this flight was filled with blue Hawaiian shirt-clad flight attendants, Hawaiian music, and the words "Aloha" and "Mahalo."

The plane landed shortly before the estimated time, and as soon as George turned off airplane mode on his phone, it rang. The Airbnb owner was on the other end of the phone line. "Aloha, welcome to Hawaii," she said. "Have you found the property yet?"

George said, "We just landed and have not even made it off the plane."

"Ok, call me when you get to the property, and I will tell you the code for the door." Answered the landlord.

At the same time George was talking with the landlord, Nadine received a message from Colton that he had arrived even earlier than anticipated and was having difficulties finding the correct baggage carousel to retrieve his luggage. It turned out that his flight had delivered him to the opposite side of the airport as his luggage, and he needed to find a way to retrieve them.

Once everyone was off the plane, Nadine and Colton spent around 20 minutes on the phone in 86-degree humid heat, trying to determine where each other was. Eventually they were able to meet up outside the car rental area. Together at last!

As they went into the car rental area, Colton told them that Luna was at her final hula practice and would not be able to get together with them until the following day.

**Rental Car.**

Back in the day, when renting a car, no one made reservations unless there was a big event going on in that city. There used to be two choices: "Avis" or "Alamo." Upon arrival at the airport, you would pick the shortest line. Both companies always had plenty of cars, whatever you wanted. Whether it was a sedan, mid-size, or compact, if they had it, you could rent it. They had plenty of cars on hand, but on the rare occasion your request was not available, the company would offer you a free upgrade and honor the price that had been quoted. They even had coupons!

After making your request, the agent would pick up the corded phone and call downstairs to "Scooter," who would verify the car's existence and pull it up to the curb. Then he would do a walk around and make sure you were comfortable with the vehicle and the options it came with.

As time passed and rental car agencies grew (There must be a company for every letter in the alphabet at this point), the process of renting a car became easier. More recently you are told to follow a marked pathway to a labeled area and just "select a vehicle." There is no walk-around. The keys are in the visor, and you are expected to select a vehicle that fits your needs.

You are then expected to do your own walk around, take photos of any blemishes you notice on the vehicle, and be on your way. This is a terrific way to drive a model of a car that you find attractive and decide if it will make a good future vehicle in your life.

On this trip, they had made a reservation for a mid-size sedan six months in advance. Upon arrival at the rental car kiosk, they encountered a line of about twenty people waiting to rent a car. While

George and Martha waited in line, Colton and Nadine made up for lost time apart by chastising and teasing each other. Finally getting their turn at the service counter, they were greeted by a woman who must have been older than the airport itself and probably used to be employed by one of the two "A's" back in the day. She wore a purple pantsuit, and had her glasses perched on the end of her nose attached with a black cord around her neck. After the woman reviewed George and Martha's identification and insurance, she removed her glasses from her nose and allowed them to rest on her chest. She looked at the couple and asked if George would be the only driver. They said no, Martha would be splitting the driving duties. The lady then informed them that if they wanted to have more than one driver it would be an additional $20 a day. This fact caused them to pause and reflect on their lives at the current moment and if they really needed a car at all!

After deciding that they indeed did need reliable transportation while on the island, they played another rousing game of rock, paper, and scissors. George lost the shot, and they decided that he would be driving for the duration of the visit. They were then given instructions to follow the escalators down to the car level and were told the car would be waiting for them.

George, Martha, Nadine, and Colton gathered their belongings and headed to the escalators. The large yellow signs saying "No luggage on escalators" caused them to redirect to the elevators. After waiting an additional five minutes, the elevator doors finally slid open. They loaded up and made the excruciating thirty-second trip down to the street level. The group exited the elevator and looked at the sign pointing them to the correct area where they were to take delivery of the mid-size sedan. There was another older couple in front of them at this point, as they had ignored the "No luggage on escalators" sign and gotten to street level moments before.

There was a young lady dressed in capri pants and a Hawaiian print shirt directing people to their vehicles. She pointed to the older couple and then pointed to a mid-size sedan suitable for up to six passengers. She then looked at George and Martha's crew, with all their luggage, and said, "Here is a car for you," pointing them to a Hyundai Elantra. The Elantra was a silver-colored four-door sedan suitable for up to four mid-size passengers.

After loading and reloading the luggage in the trunk, playing a game of car luggage Tetris with their bags, they decided that Martha and Nadine would have to hold two of the carry-ons on their laps while George drove, and Colton took the role of navigator.

Once Martha and Nadine were settled into their seats, George and Colton filmed a quick video of the outside of the vehicle in the event the company attempted to charge them for damage done before their use of the vehicle. They paused in their task and watched enviously as the older couple effortlessly tossed their baggage into the trunk of their true mid-size sedan, climbed in, and drove away. Lucky Bums!

George and Colton climbed down into the vehicle, adjusted the seats, turned on the air conditioner, and then they were on their way! Straight into the line to exit the garage. Because of the building construction, the GPS spun out of control until they finally exited the garage. The bright Hawaiian sun nearly blinded them as they fumbled to pull the visors down and find the sign directing them to the highway. Anticipating freeway speeds, they merged into traffic and turned up the air conditioning fan. As soon as they got to an even flowing pace, they hit rush hour traffic. Colton said, "Our exit is only a mile ahead, but the GPS says it will take us 20 minutes to get there". At that point, they elected to turn off the air conditioning and roll down all four windows.

Eventually, they made their way to the exit, and following the GPS and Colton's directions, they found the appropriate side roads leading to the Airbnb. The car nearly bottomed out as they flew through the intersection and began the ascent up the road to the property. Suddenly, Colton shouted, "There it is!" George slammed on the brakes, causing Martha and Nadine's heads to slam forward, forcing their chins into their chests and then back against the headrests as he determined how to navigate the driveway. Having a quick break in the traffic, George hit the gas, once again causing the three passengers' heads to flop back and forth. As quickly as he had punched the gas, he hit the brakes again, lurching to a stop avoiding making physical contact with the building in the small driveway.

As soon as the car came to a stop, George's phone rang again. "Aloha, welcome to the property!" the landlord said. "You will be in the house downstairs. Once you get to the door, I will tell you the code to open it".

Martha and Nadine exited the vehicle, rubbing their necks and mumbling sarcastically to each other that they were glad George lost the game and would be driving the rest of the trip. As they began to unload the car and load Colton's arms, George went down the stairs in front of where he had parked and said into his phone, "Ok, where do I go? I am down by the laundry."

The landlord said, "That is the wrong house. Go back upstairs and go the other way." It was not until he made it back to the parking area that George saw another set of stairs leading to a patio area and another entry. As he glanced up, George noticed several CCTV cameras at the doorways of all the entries.

He looked up at the camera and said, "This one?"

The landlord said, "Yes! Here is the code."

While George fumbled with the code, Colton came down the stairs, arms full of luggage, followed by Martha and Nadine, also loaded down with carry-ons and backpacks.

After approximately eighteen attempts at the code, due to traffic noise, the door was successfully opened!

The Airbnb was painted brown, with white trim, and had a cement porch entryway with a brown-trimmed railing. One had to walk down a set of three cement steps across a shared patio area lined with rock leading up to the street to access the front door of the house.

They made their way into the house and were met with the smell of humid heat in the air. The front door opened into the living room area. To the right was a small staircase to nowhere that ended with a locked door. Continuing straight, there was a long hallway that led to the kitchen located in the back of the house. To the right of the hallway were two bedrooms and two bathrooms, while on the left were the other two bedrooms.

Everyone selected a bedroom, and the search for the thermostat to turn the air conditioning down began. After a short search of all the rooms, Martha looked at the reviews of the property in more detail, and it was then discovered that there was NO air conditioning, only ceiling fans and two tall stand fans, one in the hallway and one in a bedroom.

The sun was shining through the windows on one side of the house so they decided they would close the curtains on that side to block some of the heat out. As it turned out the plan changed because there were only see-through bits of sheer fabric hanging in all the rooms, and not a curtain to be found. All the windows were quickly opened, as well as the front and back doors, and fans were relocated to other areas of the house in an attempt to maximize airflow.

The afternoon had flown by since they had landed on the island, and everyone was getting what the Rainier family considered hangry.

They decided to go shopping and gather some supplies and food for the week. When they had previously been on the island in 2018, they had gone to Walmart for groceries and decided that would be the best bet to get what they needed for this trip. George climbed into the driver's seat, Colton fired up his GPS from the passenger seat, and they made their way towards downtown Honolulu.

The wind blew through everyone's hair as they streaked down the street towards the downtown corridor. They had decided to leave the air conditioning off in the car and lower all the windows in an attempt to enjoy the tropical weather of the islands.

The GPS led them straight to the downtown Walmart and into the parking garage. They began the ascent into the parking garage. As they wound in a counterclockwise direction, Colton said, "Dad, the wall is getting really close over here!" This comment caused George to chuckle and tighten his grip on the steering wheel.

George continued the climb up into the parking lot. When they emerged into the blinding daylight, they came to a flat area with a single arm gate. There was a sign on a keypad box before the gate that read, 'This Walmart is permanently closed.' Under that sign was a plate disclosing a parking rates fee schedule and instructions saying, "Take a ticket to enter."

After pondering their situation and determining that there was no way to turn around, they decided they didn't want to pay the eight dollars for the pleasure of driving through the abandoned parking lot. George called the telephone number that was on the keypad in hopes of finding help. The voice on the other end informed them that they could indeed enter the abandoned lot, and as long as they made it to the exit on the main level within five minutes, there would be no charge.

Challenge accepted! George took the ticket, the gate arm raised, and he hit the gas while the theme song from the "Dukes of Hazzard" ran through his head. The passengers' necks were once again thrust backward as they began the clockwise descent through the parking lot, as Colton echoed his earlier comment about the wall getting awfully close! The group made their way to the exit of the garage within a record-breaking three minutes. They were looked at disgustedly by the garage personnel, who allowed them to exit the garage without paying a fee. As they merged onto the main road, the song "Eastbound and Down" began to run through George's head.

Unbeknownst to them, they passed right by the grocery store Safeway and made their way to Costco. The family wandered around Costco for a while, enjoying the air conditioning, and pointed out items that they could not get at their local Costco stores. They purchased a few breakfast items as well as some food for dinner that night.

As they prepared to exit Costco's parking lot, Colton suddenly said, "Hey, look, a kitty." Everyone looked in the direction he was pointing and noticed a large number of cats that had a residence in the parking lot. After several awe's and loving comments about the strays, George turned the car out of the parking lot.

They made their way back to the house and were greeted with a marvelous Hawaiian sunset. Because the islands are located so close to the equator, the sun sets at the same time every evening, so the family made a note of when that time was so that they could try and enjoy the sunset every night.

The car windows were rolled down again and the Rainers enjoyed the pleasant tropical evening, looking forward to how many more evenings they would get to enjoy on this trip.

Deciding to make it easier on themselves for the next day, George backed into the driveway from the main road, stopping just before making contact with the potted plants that adorned the area.

They had dinner in the kitchen and quickly discovered the light above the table was failing as it was blinking at such a speed that everyone was worried someone could potentially fall into an epileptic seizure. Martha made a mental note that when she texted a request for fresh towels, she would add a light bulb to the list.

An attempt to use the microwave resulted in the discovery that one had to close the door securely and lift one corner of the unit, place their tongue against the roof of their mouth, and cross their big toes over their second toes on each foot in order for it to operate.

After their makeshift meal, they all unpacked their bags settling into their rooms. Everyone finally got to bed around 11:00 pm Hawaii time. This would have been 2:00 am George, Martha, and Nadine's time and 5:00 am Colton's time. It had been a long day for all of them, but especially Colton who had a six-hour time difference from when he had left Ohio that morning.

Around 2:00 am, George's phone chimed with a text notification. George fumbled with his glasses and saw that the landlord had texted asking him to park closer to the green bushes on the side of the driveway in order to allow other vehicles to park in the lot. After reading this message, George took off his glasses and placed them along with his phone back on the dresser. He looked at the time and thought, '*What a crazy time to be texting!*'

Since they were both awake, Martha and George decided to use the restroom. They went into the hallway, and Martha heard a strange sound. Working her way into the kitchen, she heard what sounded like people talking coming through the open window. "George, come here," said Martha. "Do you hear that?" George came into the kitchen rubbing his tired eyes, and although he did not have his hearing aids in, he could still clearly hear what sounded like muffled voices talking. The voices seemed to be coming from the neighboring house.

Thinking it was just someone listening to a podcast or a recording, they ignored it and went back to bed.

The next morning, when they came into the kitchen, the voices were still talking. The mysterious phenomenon continued constantly during their trip, and they never found out what or who it was.

# Wednesday

There comes a time in anyone's life when suddenly they realize that they are adults and they must make adult decisions.

This realization was driven through George on the first full day of their trip.

Everyone woke up early because of the time zone differences in their lives. Martha, Colton, and Nadine had the entire day planned out. They were going to begin the day by watching the sunrise, but plans changed because it was raining.

They planned to go to a sandwich shop on their way to the Dole plantation. After the Dole plantation they planned to stop at the poke' shack and get lunch to go. Before heading to the beach for a day of relaxation, the group would make a stop for some shaved ice.

Their first stop, however, would be coffee!

They all gathered to help prepare a quick breakfast before they began the day's adventures. Martha took the frozen breakfast sandwiches they had purchased from Costco from the freezer, separated them so that they would warm evenly, placed the egg and sausage on a plate, and handed the plate to Colton.

Colton's job was to warm the contents of the plate. Colton repeatedly slammed the door to the microwave, lifted up the corner, and held the machine level while it warmed the food.

Martha toasted the bread portion of the sandwiches. After being toasted, the bread was handed to George to butter and add any condiments that were requested from the others on the bread. The bread plate was then passed to Nadine, who was seated next to Colton.

Colton pulled the plate from the microwave and placed the now-warmed egg, sausage, and cheese on the toasted bread. Nadine then distributed the completed breakfast to each person. This scenario continued through the week.

Martha and George were cleaning up the dishes when Luna arrived bearing a gift of home-grown apple bananas. Luna explained to George and Martha that apple bananas are smaller-sized bananas that are primarily grown in tropical areas. They tend to have a sweeter, tangier flavor along with a faint pineapple, strawberry, or apple flavor.

While they had previously talked on the phone and video chatted, until today, George and Martha had never met Luna face-to-face, and they were looking forward to their time together.

Luna decided that Colton would be riding with her because the rental car was not large enough to fit everyone comfortably. They all loaded into their assigned vehicles and drove down the hill to the closest Starbucks. Parking in the shade, they exited the vehicles and were about to go in and place their order when Martha realized she had left her phone back at the house. She needed it in order to earn her reward points.

George and Martha left the "kids" (if you can call 22 and 24-year-olds kids) in the parking lot and drove back up the hill to the Airbnb to retrieve her phone.

After entering the code on the front door and waving to the landlord via the CCTV camera, Martha secured her phone, and they descended the hill back to the coffee shop.

While they were waiting for George and Martha to return, Colton discovered that if he were to gently tug on a tree branch, it would cause a unique sound to be made as it dripped the water from the rainstorm earlier that day and splashed off of the car. He also discovered that he could potentially soak the girls from the water running off the leaves and found great delight in doing just that! Nadine retaliated by hitting the trunk of the tree and causing even more water to drop on them all. Luna reacted with a resounding "Hey, Excuse you…Rude!" All the while, Colton and Nadine were laughing because the water felt refreshing.

George and Martha pulled back into the parking lot, found a shady spot to park, and rejoined the others. They went into the Starbucks, and all placed their order. When complete, they took hold of their drinks, loaded into their assigned seats, and were off to the North Shore for a day of fun, sun, and relaxation. There was a massive accident on the freeway, which caused traffic to move very slowly. Luna and George navigated through the traffic, and George even earned some kudos from Nadine for navigating the lanes so smoothly.

They made their way to Kapolei. Luna had taken Colton and Nadine to this city the year before and had discovered a sandwich shop that they wanted George and Martha to experience. Luna said that there was no street parking available but that they could park in the Jack-in-the-Box parking lot and walk to the deli.

They backed into side-by-side parking spaces at the Jack in the Box restaurant. They parked next to a large black truck. As they exited the vehicles and locked the doors, George looked over at the truck and noticed that it had a sign on it that said, "K9 Unit, Do Not Approach." Thinking it was a police officer, he made a mental note to thank them for their service when they returned to the restaurant to order some food.

As they walked by the Jack in the Box drive-through, George noticed a sign that said, "No bills over $20," and told Martha that they needed to break a large bill in order to order when they returned.

It was about a two-block walk to the sandwich shop. They were inside the deli for about ten minutes. Everyone placed their order, and George noticed several handwritten cardboard signs that said, "If you park at Jack in the Box, you will be towed!" He got nervous after reading this warning multiple times throughout the sandwich shop. George paid the bill and asked Colton if they would wait for the sandwiches while he and Martha walked back to the vehicles. Now that they had some smaller bills, George and Martha thought that when they got back to Jack-in-the-box, they would order a salad to enhance their lunches.

As George and Martha came around the corner, George glanced between two buildings into the parking lot just in time to see the big black truck with the K9 warning on it towing Luna's car out of the parking lot and disappearing into the alley across the street. Shaking his head and rubbing his eyes, George looked for the rental car and noticed it was already gone! George and Martha both raced into the restaurant and told the man behind the counter, "We went to get change to come back and order some food, and you towed our vehicles?!"

The man behind the counter said in broken English, "We have nothing to do with it; it's all the towing company. Can I take your order?"

George said, "You really think we are going to order something now after you had our vehicles towed?!"

The man said, "You have to call the number on the sign." and pointed to the parking lot on the other side of the building.

George and Martha stormed out of the restaurant and were immediately surrounded by people from neighboring businesses, all asking if their vehicles had been towed.

"It is a scam! And Jack-in-the-box is in on it!" Exclaimed one man.

Another said, "I wish you would have parked in my lot; I wouldn't have done that to you."

A third man said, "This happened to me a few days ago. A group of us are gathering our resources to sue the restaurant and the towing company. You will have to pay to get the vehicles back, but here is my contact information."

George pulled out his phone and called the number on the sign. The lady who answered verified that both the vehicles were there and said it would cost around $135 to have them released. George asked if the total was for both vehicles, and she responded, "Yes." She gave the address of where to claim the cars. It was about a six-block walk to the towing company. She suggested getting an Uber to get there, but they determined that by the time the Uber even showed up, they could walk to the towing yard.

Realization hit George again that he was the adult in this situation. He decided to pull the cash to bail out the vehicles from his wallet and have it in his pocket to make the transaction faster, and so that the receptionist would not see the contents of his wallet. And to top off the horror of the situation, their Starbucks drinks were still in the rental car and melting!

The walk to the towing yard was brutal because they had not planned on spending time outdoors yet. No one had applied sunscreen. George was wearing flip-flops in anticipation of spending a day on the beach. Nadine managed to sunburn, and George worked a blister on the top of his foot, but the adrenaline he had pumping through his system because of the anger he was carrying did not notice it right away.

Halfway there, Colton said, "Luna's dad cannot hear about this. I do not know what we would have done if you had not been here" (More adulting for George).

They arrived at the towing yard and quickly noticed both vehicles parked in a fenced area. There was a break in the fence, and two 55-gallon barrels served as the service counter for bailing out the impounded vehicles.

The towing yard man with a toothpick in the corner of his mouth sauntered over and asked if he could help them. George said that both of their vehicles had been towed, and he would like them back. The man said, "Just a moment," and walked through a roll-up door and pretended to speak with someone inside the former service station.

The man returned with a slip of paper in his hand and verbally gave the total that would enable the vehicles to be freed. It was double what the lady had quoted over the phone! George told the man how much he had been quoted. The man answered, "Yes, for each vehicle."

When asked if they took credit cards, the man answered "No" but he informed George that there was an ATM in the adjoining office with only a $7 surcharge.

George thrust his hand into his pocket and withdrew his wallet, taking the last of the cash he had on hand and handing it to the man said "I want a receipt with your address on it so my attorney can contact you. Can we get our vehicles now?"

The man said, "Ok, one at a time, come get your vehicles." George started to say that Luna was the driver of the other vehicle, but the man stopped him, saying, "One at a time."

George climbed into the rental car and pulled out of the fenced area. His only choice was to pull into the parking lot next door and then return to the towing yard and drive the other vehicle out. When he parked the rental in an open spot, he looked up and saw the signs indicating that if they parked there, they would be towed.

"Someone come sit in this car so I can get the other one, please!" George demanded. Martha was heading to the car to make sure it was occupied when George saw Luna driving her vehicle out of the fenced area.

As everyone loaded back into the vehicles, Martha shouted to the man, "Thanks for taking all of our vacation cash!" The man turned his back to the group, waved one hand over his head, dismissing her words, and disappeared through the roll-up door.

George looked down at his foot and saw the blood pooling from the blister he had gained during their walk to the towing yard. He slipped the flip-flop off and drove barefoot to the Dole plantation, planning to tend to it when they arrived.

On the way, George told Martha, "I've got to shake this off. I cannot let this ruin the rest of our trip" Martha agreed and suggested that he find a tree to release his negative energy into because George was slightly spiritual.

When they arrived at the Dole plantation, George attempted to walk to Luna's vehicle, but the pain from the blister finally reared its ugly head and stopped him in his tracks. Nadine swapped shoes with George so that he could continue the trek to Luna's vehicle, where she had a first aid kit. Luna gave George a bandage that he placed over the blister.

As they exited the parking area, everyone scanned the poles, looking for signs indicating 'no parking' zones. Seeing that they both were legally parked, they made their way into the plantation's gift shop.

George and Martha walked around while the kids did some souvenir shopping. George and Martha bought a Dole whip to share and made their way to a table with an umbrella just outside of the building. They were beginning to relax again, enjoying the warm Hawaiian air. Finishing their treat, George looked over towards the little train that took people on tours. He noticed the entry was surrounded by palm trees and said, "See that palm tree? I am going to lay hands on it and expel the negative energy."

Martha answered him with, "Don't make the tree fall on the train." George stepped through the garden bed and placed his hands on the tree, grounding himself and thanking the tree for taking the negative energy and dispersing it.

Returning to the table he had been sharing with Martha, he noticed their group had all gathered to enjoy their tropical treat and were huddled under the umbrella in an attempt to avoid the light drizzle that had begun. There were several feral cats on the property, and being animal people, everyone tried talking to them in an attempt to pet them and see if they would reward the group with a sweet meow.

Martha gained the attention of one cat in particular. She was talking nicely to it, and it slowly approached her, tail high in the air, and looked as if it might come to her. Suddenly, the cat looked at her and gagged, almost retching in front of them. Everyone laughed as they attempted to shake off the negative feeling from the towing experience earlier.

After their snack, they continued north to obtain poke' bowls before they continued to the beach. George, Martha, and Nadine missed the turn to the poke' bowl shack and had to continue several miles before being able to turn around and finally meet back up with Luna and Colton.

The poke' shack was closed, and Nadine was heartbroken. They continued further down the road until they reached a small village with a lot of food trucks.

They parked the vehicles in a parking lot behind the storefronts of the little village and left Nadine and Colton to stay with the vehicles in case the greedy tow truck decided to come around again.

While Luna, George, and Martha ventured to find food for Martha to eat, Colton and Nadine noticed some chickens that were wandering the parking lot. They began to harass the poor poultry and wound up chasing them into the foliage adjacent to the parking lot.

After successfully finding Martha some lunch, they regrouped, and all went to have shaved ice. This required moving the vehicles again, as the food trucks were on the opposite end of the village from the shaved ice shack.

They parked in a lot within walking distance of the shaved ice shack, checked again for 'no parking' zones, and walked across the street to place their orders. George and Martha split a pina colada flavored ice. Colton and Luna shared a cotton candy flavored treat while Nadine enjoyed a strawberry vanilla all to herself.

While enjoying the frozen treat, some friendly geckos, in the process of changing color from their natural green color to the dark blue color of the shaved ice shack, joined them.

As they walked back to the vehicles, Colton and Nadine were having fun swinging Luna between them like a child. They each grasped one of her arms, lifted Luna off the ground, and swung her back and forth. Everyone laughed as Luna said, "Again!" and they continued the short walk back to their vehicles to continue their journey to the beach.

They arrived at the parking lot for the beach and made their way through the grassy area towards the beach. The trail through the dune opened to reveal light brown sands, blue waters, and lots of coral. After multiple trips to the car, they set up a dining canopy for shade against the tropical sun, lathered on sunscreen, and attempted to relax. The kids spread their towels and mats out under the canopy while George and Martha attempted to set up lawn chairs to sit in. The possibility of leveling the chairs against the slope of the beach was almost nonexistent, and every time the sun moved, so did the group.

Luna played some Hawaiian music over the Bluetooth speaker, adding to the tropical atmosphere.

Once their makeshift camp was set up, they dove into the sandwiches and the carne asada Martha had purchased from the food truck. With their bellies full again, they all sat back and tried to relax under the canopy.

At one point, George found a unique piece of coral buried in the sand. He considered keeping it as a souvenir, but he remembered an episode of the Brady Bunch when the Brady kids brought back a curse from the islands. After their experience with the towing company earlier that day, he opted to take a photo with his phone and then threw the coral into the water.

The waterline was far too rough with coral to allow swimming, so everyone decided to wade instead. There were a few kite surfers that they enjoyed watching, their boards bouncing off the top of the waves, causing them to fly several feet in the air and land, only to become airborne again as they traveled down the coastline.

Several helicopters circled the beach while they were there, drowning out the sound of waves crashing on the coral. A joke was made by the group that the helicopters contained the tow truck driver looking for them.

As the sun went down, the weather changed. It started to rain lightly. They enjoyed the sight of a double rainbow. As the rain picked up, so did the wind. Everyone gathered their resources and energy to collapse the canopy, stuffed their belongings in any bag they could find, and made the trek back to the vehicles.

On the way back to the parking lot, they noticed that there were little thorny plants that the Rainiers called goat heads, growing in the grass and the thorns that had collected in their shoes. They needed to be plucked out before getting into the vehicles. George lifted the ice chest into the trunk with a loud thunk, and approximately half of the sand from the beach that had been attached to it fell off onto the carpeting in the trunk of the rental car. They were thankful that the sand had landed in the car and not the house, as the house had a zero-sand policy.

They began their journey back to the Airbnb and made a stop at a different Wal-Mart on the way. Nadine had realized she was even more burned than before because she "forgot" to put on sunscreen. It was determined that she needed to purchase some t-shirts to cover her freshly scorched skin for the rest of the trip, as she had only packed tank tops.

That weekend was Mother's Day, and as they walked through the store, George snapped his fingers and pointed to the card aisle (adulting), where Nadine and Colton dutifully disappeared for a while to pick out a card for Martha. Nadine also selected some seaweed salad to eat later since she wasn't able to get poke' earlier in the day. Colton hefted a case of bottled water to restock the refrigerator, and they returned to the Airbnb, arriving close to 10:00 pm. Luna dropped off Colton and had to return to her home because of the curfew set in place by the Airbnb's landlord.

After unloading their belongings, Colton decided to take a shower while George and Nadine watched a murder mystery program. Suddenly Martha screamed! George looked at Nadine and said, "I've never heard that noise come out of her before."

He quickly got up and rushed down the hall towards where he had heard the noise. A "B52" cockroach, also known as a flying cockroach, had run between Martha's legs and was headed to the other bedroom. George picked up a garbage can and set it down on the roach hard! Killing it.

After searching the house for something to sweep it up, George took the decorative broom from the wall, found a dustpan, and cleaned up the mess as best he could. Then, hung the broom back up, praying that the landlord would not notice the dangling cockroach legs and wings stuck in the broom's bristles.

Everyone had regrouped in the living room. The lights were off, and they were watching television. The doors were open with the screen doors closed and a nice breeze had begun flowing through the hallway. The traffic noise had settled down for the night and they were feeling relaxed, starting to cool off and discussing their plans for the next day.

Suddenly, movement caught everyone's attention as another B52 flew under the screen and into the house.

George grabbed the decorative broom and the dustpan and attempted to swat it out of the air and get it out of the house, but it flew down the stairway to nowhere and under the mysteriously locked door.

Martha made a comment about how that roach had better not end up in bed with them!

With that statement, and everyone has had enough stress for one day, doors were closed as tightly as they could be and everyone went to bed.

It had been about thirty minutes since George and Martha had gone to bed, all the lights were out and it was warm because of no air conditioning and having to close the doors. Suddenly, Martha felt her hair fall on her neck and went to brush it away, but it had a hard shell and moved! The roach had indeed found its way into the bed and was crawling on her neck.

Martha screamed and jumped (literally) out of bed. George got out of bed and said, "Get me the broom," as he tried to brush it out of the bed with his hand onto the floor.

Martha grabbed the broom from the wall and yelled for Colton, saying, "Colton, get in here and help your dad!"

Colton said, "What am I supposed to do?"

Martha replied, "I don't know, just help!"

Nadine quietly closed her bedroom door in hopes that the others would think she was sleeping and would not enlist her help.

George managed to trap the roach in the dustpan and told Colton to open the door; they threw the roach outside, slammed it, and locked the door. The broom was hung on the wall once again. George noticed the leg and wings from the first assault were missing and made a quick check of the bed to ensure that they were not there.

After a full day of adulting, everyone was exhausted. Luna had an early morning planned for them the next day, and they were going to have to get up early. Eventually everyone was able to fall back to sleep, determined to have a more relaxing day tomorrow.

Aloha-
Ha!

# Thursday

Rise and Shine! Adventure time! Their plan for the morning was to do a sunrise hike to see the Makapu'u lighthouse. Everyone got up at 3:00 am Hawaii time, which was 6:00 am Washington's time and 9:00 am Ohio's time. It was raining…and the mysterious talking was still audible from the neighbor through the open window.

Nadine emerged from the bathroom and was not feeling well. She sat on one of the chairs in the living room and took some deep breaths in an attempt to calm the nausea that raged in her belly. She drank a bottle of water and decided to suck it up and try to enjoy the day.

Luna showed up at the Airbnb at 5:00 am. Once again, they utilized both vehicles. Following Luna through the neighborhood pre-dawn turned out to be an interesting decision. They missed a few turns, went through some residential areas, and had to make a couple of U-turns. All of this driving activity was doing nothing to help settle Nadine's stomach. Eventually, they arrived at the park where the lighthouse was located.

Fortunately for them, the rain had stopped before they reached the park entrance. It was early enough that the park gate was still closed and locked, making the parking lot not accessible. Other early risers had parked their vehicles alongside the road, and the automobile occupants were walking around the locked gate to access the path that led to the lookout over the lighthouse.

Luna pulled off the road into a nice wide spot with just enough room for her vehicle to fit. George pulled ahead a little further, and

Martha had to get out of the rental car so that George could snug the car as close to the ditch as possible without either falling in the ditch or colliding with the road sign that he was attempting to park beside. Rolling both windows down, turning off the radio, and listening as intently as he could, they got the car parked. He set the brake while they grabbed their backpacks and then secured the car.

George checked the sign that he had parked next to, making sure that it was not a parking prohibited area. He wiped his eyes to clear them of any residual sleep blinked. Using the flashlight on his phone, he checked the sign again. George also scanned every single sign in the immediate area, ensuring that they were parked as legally as they could be, and then rejoined the group to begin their ascent up the mountain.

After walking around the locked gate, there was about a quarter-mile walk through the parking lot to the trailhead. The sky was starting to change to a bright blue color, and they feared they would not make it to the top before sunrise.

Nadine glanced anxiously at the locked restrooms as they began the hike and decided she was feeling okay enough to join the group who was already beginning their trek up the trail.

The Rainer family had observed that on the island of Oahu, the police cars were easily identifiable during dark hours because of the blue lights that were constantly lit as they ran their patrol routes. George watched anxiously every time a police car drove past the locked parking lot, knowing there was nothing they could do if the police officers decided that their car should not be parked where it was. Even just being partially up the trail, he would never make it back in time in the event the police decided to tow it. Fortunately, their cars were not the only ones parked in that manner, and Luna assured them that people parked that way all the time. This did nothing to calm George's apprehension as he remembered her saying the same thing prior to them parking at Jack in the Box the day before.

The paved trail continued at a steep grade with very few level places to stop (like three) and very few switchbacks to alleviate their sore and tired feet. They continued their climb. Stopping several times to catch their breath and take gulps of water. When they were about three-quarters of the way to the top, they paused and observed the sun rising over the mighty Pacific Ocean.

Once the sun had risen above the water level, they continued their ascent. They reached the top of the trail and were able to look down on the lighthouse. They watched the water crashing on the rocks and imagined that they could hear mermaids singing below, enticing them to be "part of their world." The group asked some people to take several photos of them so they could prove to the world via social media that they had indeed made the trek and survived.

As they began their descent, the mermaid's song suddenly became real, especially for Nadine. The sounds became much louder and more intense. It sounded more like Ursula had come to the surface to see what the human world was all about!

After pausing to listen to Ursula's angry tune, it occurred to them that the noise was actually Nadine's stomach. The seaweed salad she had consumed the night before had not liked the climb and wanted to remain at the top of the trail. No one had any antacids on them; why would they? This was a sunrise hike, rewarded with coffee and breakfast once they made it back down and into town. Fortunately for Nadine, Martha had some peppermint candies in her backpack, and

Nadine sucked on the candies while Martha rubbed her back and tried to talk her down from retching like the cat from the previous day.

After a bit of peppermint and some water, they were able to slowly continue their descent towards the vehicles, which were located outside of the now unlocked parking lot.

On the way down the path, Luna kept chasing birds, saying they were not real and were only there to spy on them! George took his time going down as his shoes were beginning to give him fits. He decided to walk with Nadine as she was walking at a slower pace, still recovering from the seaweed salad and mermaid song duet.

Once everyone was gathered at the bottom of the trail, they talked about their next stop for the day. They took a group photo in front of the park's sign, and Luna being Luna, laid at the base of the sign and acted as if she were holding up the letters with all her might.

They made their short trek back to the vehicles, and Luna climbed into the driver's seat of her car while Colton guided her out of the precarious parking place. Martha guided George in a similar fashion. Everyone claimed their appropriate places in the vehicles, and they were off to their next stop for the day's adventures.

After a distance of less than a mile, they stopped at Makapu'u Beach Park to use the restrooms. The restrooms were located at the top of a rock staircase. From this vantage point, they were able to enjoy another perspective of the lighthouse and see the top of the mountain they had just climbed. They encouraged their already wobbly legs so that they could climb just a few more steps. Soon, they were refreshed and back in the vehicles, headed towards town in search of food.

Their next stop was Waimanalo Beach Park where they planned to have a picnic breakfast. They legally parked both vehicles and walked (more walking!) across a muddy field to the 7-11 to purchase some breakfast food.

They purchased spam musubi (seaweed-wrapped Spam and Rice), Lup cheong manapua (Chinese sausage surrounded with sweet bread), and other goodies that would help them get through the day. Again, Luna found herself chasing the pigeons as everyone else walked precariously (trying not to slide through the muddy grass), all while giving a wide berth to the homeless people who inhabited the park.

Once they were back in the park, they secured a picnic table, and everyone satisfied their appetites with the goodies they had purchased. Nadine was feeling better at this point and was able to take nourishment as well. Martha was kind enough to share her breakfast with some of the birds that Luna had stopped chasing for the time being.

The sand and water at this park were picture-perfect and they took the time to snap several photos, enjoying the cool breeze that blew through the park. They turned around and gazed at the lush green hills and were amazed to see that it was raining at the higher elevation. This allowed them to view several beautiful waterfalls that were cascading down the mountains.

Deciding that they should eat their way through the day again, their next stop was the Waiahole Poi Factory. After purchasing lunch to go, they returned to their vehicles with their arms full of bags of warm food that emitted the enticing smells of chicken, roasted pork, salmon, and the earthy aroma of the taro leaves. They also bought

"My Sweet Lady of Waiahole (taro and ice cream)" and had to eat it quickly for fear that it would melt.

As they approached the parking lot, they discovered that they were not the only ones who knew how to park precariously. Someone had parked so close to Luna's vehicle that she had to enter the vehicle through the back hatch door and use her skills as a hula dancer to maneuver up and around the seats like a ninja, eventually landing in the driver's seat. She then backed the car out of the space far enough for Colton to climb into the passenger seat. Luckily, no paint was exchanged between either vehicle.

Luna then led the caravan of two to the Tropical Farms Macadamia Nut Factory. In the parking lot, they were lucky enough to observe a mother hen and her fuzz-covered chicks. The beautiful brown mother hen hurried her fluffy yellow and black chicks from place to place. Nadine, who was feeling a lot better, was videoing them and asking them not to attack her. Luna slowly snuck up behind Nadine and yelled loud enough to startle her. Nadine screamed aloud and nearly dropped her phone as she reached out to keep herself from falling forward to the ground. This caused the chicks to seek refuge with their mother and scamper into the trees. Luna laughed so hard that she was soon doubled over at the thought of startling her friend.

Inside the store, they sampled several diverse kinds of nuts, coffees, and lotions. After a few handfuls of the garlic-flavored nuts, vampires were no longer a concern for the group. They opted not to crack open any nuts as George had a flashback to a previous trip to the farm where the chickens stood ready to steal any nuts that were not claimed fast enough by the humans.

While they were browsing through the shop and picking out postcards to send to Colton's twin sister, Martha saw a sample lotion that claimed to help ease sunburn pain. Martha got Nadine's attention and had her come over to the shelf. Martha squirted some lotion into her hand and gently massaged it into Nadine's badly sunburned arm.

After they were done shopping, again loading their arms with all sorts of treasures and souvenirs, they again returned to their vehicles and continued to Kualoa Beach Park to eat the food that they had purchased from the poi factory. The park was on the water's edge, and looking out, you could see Mokoli'I, also known as Chinaman's hat, the same island displayed in the intro scenes of the old television show Gilligan's Island. Looking in the other direction they observed the beautiful green mountainous area where the movie Jurassic Park had been filmed. Because of the recent rains, they were able to observe several more waterfalls flowing over the green mountains, adding to the beauty of the day. They shared some grains of rice with some attractive local birds that had bright red heads and some beautiful white egrets. Luna was too tired to chase these birds and let them eat in peace.

Having had such an early start to the day, the mainlanders were tired and decided to head back to the house for some much-needed rest. They decided to take a different route that went through the middle of the island and a mountain instead of the road that had taken them around that morning.

Halfway back to the Airbnb, Nadine suddenly said, "MOM!"

Startled, Martha said, "What?"

Nadine said, "Just look at my arm where you put the lotion!" It was quite visible that where Martha had spread the lotion on Nadine's arm, it had begun to heal. One could even see marks from Martha's fingers where she had stopped spreading the balm.

Arriving at the Airbnb, everyone decided that a nap would be in order. The doors were closed to avoid any unwanted B52 action, and they all slept for a few hours. When everyone awoke, the decision was made that they should probably eat… again. George did not want to drive anymore, so Colton and Luna placed an order at Zippy's restaurant and brought back food for everyone.

After the meal, George took the garbage out to the curbside cans, and almost immediately, his phone rang. It was the landlord of the Airbnb telling him that he put the garbage in the wrong can and he should go back outside, remove the bag from the container he had placed it in, and place it in the correct one!

A short time later, everyone was craving something sweet. Luna and Colton made yet another trip to the store, this time enlisting the help of Nadine, and brought back ice cream.

With full bellies and not-so-nice weather, the group decided to lounge in front of the television and watch some movies. Taking advantage of the downtime, they talked and planned out the next few days. Luna was sure to keep her eye on the clock and left around 9:45 to avoid any additional unnecessary texts or calls from the landlord.

The Rainiers did a quick once over of the house, making sure they would not have any unwanted guests and retired for the night.

# Friday

At the University of Hawaii-Manoa, it is customary for the graduating class to have a convocation ceremony the day before graduation.

The Rainiers, being unfamiliar with the word "convocation," asked Nadine to look up the definition. She grabbed her phone, did a search for the word, and said, "According to the Oxford dictionary, convocation is a large formal assembly of people."

Before the assembly, Luna wanted to put together a short video and create a poster board to remember her time in college. She implored Colton to assist with putting the video together and then asked George, Martha, and Nadine if they would help color portions of the poster board, mostly filling in the lettering that she had already outlined.

George was very adamant about making sure the poster board was the way Luna wanted. She kept saying, "Whatever you want," and then as George picked up the next color, she would teasingly say, "Not that one." While George painstakingly utilized his inner artist, Martha went back and forth from the laundry area, ensuring that they had enough clean clothes to make it through the rest of the trip

Once the video and poster board were up to Luna's standards, she quickly stowed her laptop and the poster board in her vehicle and went home to change clothes and prepare herself for the convocation.

Martha gave a quick call to the landlord and requested that they bring additional towels, some garbage bags, and a light bulb, explaining the strobe-like effect it was having on everyone every time the light was turned on.

Luna was feeling extremely nervous as she drove to the convocation. She was worried that she might be late because of the traffic and weather. Her nervous feeling continued when she pulled into the stadium parking lot and did not see any of her friends and saw the rain falling from the sky.

Luna had gotten the Rainers a parking pass, and after circling several floors, they finally found a space that could accommodate the rental car. They met up with Luna and began the walk toward the modular unit, where a reception was to take place after the convocation.

It was drizzling as they walked along the streets. There were five people and only one umbrella. Colton elected to walk with Luna, using the umbrella to guard her hair and make-up from the effects of the rain. Upon arrival at the modular unit, they all went inside and were met at the door with a blast of frigid air from the air conditioner. Because their hair and clothing were damp, it was a bit of a shock to their systems.

After dropping off the poster board and the laptop that contained the video clip, they all heaved a collective sigh before venturing out into the weather again. They continued walking to the amphitheater where the gathering would take place. The drizzle had turned into rain, and once again, Colton sheltered Luna with the umbrella.

The amphitheater was an open-air arena, and Nadine, Colton, and Martha quickly made their way to the top row of the seating area in hopes of being able to see everything. Martha had brought two plastic garbage bags to sit on, but those quickly filled with water faster than the main seating area themselves. Everyone's clothing was soaked at this point, and George had to keep running his hands through his hair to shed the water that was running like a small creek into his eyes and face. He looked around and said, "Ok, I'm done," seriously considering going back to the house and coming back later to pick everyone up.

George was trying to decide what to do when he spied on a group of trees and said, "I'm going to go stand under the trees." He quickly walked through the stadium area and found some slight relief being sheltered by the trees. Approximately three and a half minutes later he looked up to see everyone else walking in his direction. They stood at the base of the trees in a feeble attempt to avoid getting any wetter from the falling rain.

Moments before the convocation was to start, the rain stopped. Luna called Colton and told him where her parents were seated. Colton led the three of them over to Luna's family, where they were invited to sit with them. Luna's family had brought extra umbrellas and were generous enough to loan one to Martha, Nadine, and George to use in the event that it began to rain again.

Luna was finally able to meet up with her friends, and her feelings of nervousness began to pass. They began having fun as they chatted and reflected on all of the struggles and accomplishments that had brought them to this point in their lives.

Once the convocation began, Luna noticed that she was not sure how she should be feeling. The reality that she was finally graduating the next day had not fully sunk in. This was her last major college event before the graduation ceremony. She was about to begin her life as a "real" adult.

There was a beautiful hula performance during the convocation that she was very moved by because she was familiar with the chant that they were dancing to.

Umbrellas were raised and lowered many times during that event. Each time the rain stopped, everyone would lower them, and every time the umbrellas were closed, the water that had accumulated on them was transferred to the people seated in front of and behind them.

Another problem with umbrellas that was observed was that unless you are sitting directly under them, they tend to drip down onto the area outside of the umbrella. During this event, the drip zone was occupied by the people sitting in front of, behind, or beside the person holding the umbrella. There was a young boy sitting in front of the Rainers who complained to his dad that he was getting wet every time they lowered their umbrella. After making this statement, he lowered his umbrella and drenched the man sitting in front of him, causing him to blush and realize the situation was the same for everyone.

George and Nadine, while managing to keep their heads dry, had one-half of their bodies dry and the other half completely waterlogged by the end of the evening. Martha was wearing khaki pants that tended to be a bit embarrassing when soaking wet. During the ceremony, Martha reached over to put her arm on George's shoulder, felt his shirt, and said, "Man, you are soaked." Which caused everyone to laugh.

While everyone huddled under whatever umbrella they could find, Colton was unaware that the umbrella he had been holding was actually soaking Luna's dad. What a way to impress your girlfriend's dad.

By the time the ceremony ended and everyone was standing around visiting with each other, the rain had stopped. George and Luna's dad were soaked, and everyone else was laughing about the way the events of the evening had unfolded.

They all walked back to the car, squishing in their shoes and trying to dry whatever article of clothing they could. They took their assigned places in the car, and George had to turn the defroster on because everyone was so wet that the car windows were fogging up.

They made their short trip over the hill and backed into the driveway.

Upon entering the house, it was discovered that the landlord had waited until she had seen that the group had left before coming to the property. She had brought some fresh towels, closed the windows, and turned off the fans. There was no light bulb to be found, however.

Ten minutes after they had returned from the convocation, George's phone rang. It was the landlord once again. She said that her husband would be bringing over a bulb. George mentioned that it was pretty late, almost the 10:00 curfew time, and the light bulb could wait until morning.

Thirty seconds later, headlights filled the living room bright enough that the group thought the sun was beginning to rise! The landlord's husband had pulled into the driveway, left the engine to his truck running, walked up the concrete steps, and delivered the bulb. Although he wanted to install the bulb right then and there, George assured him that he could do it, so he placed the bulb in George's hand and turned to walk down the stairs. He said "Good night" over his shoulder and returned to his idling truck. He quickly backed onto the road, once again filling the living room with the bright lights, stopping briefly while he put the truck in drive and roared down the hill towards the downtown area.

George carefully placed the new bulb in the kitchen and paused to listen to the mysterious voices coming through the open window for a few moments. They all performed the new nightly ritual of making sure they would not have unwanted visitors, turned out the lights, and got ready for bed.

# Saturday

Graduation day had finally arrived! Luna was going to be extremely busy that day, so she would not be able to catch up with the Rainier family until after the ceremony.

It was a lovely day weather-wise at the Airbnb. The group had a leisurely breakfast of fresh pineapple, strawberries, and apple bananas, along with some fried sausage, eggs, and an English muffin. Everyone took their appropriate places at the table, and everyone paused to listen to the mysterious voices still coming from the neighboring window.

During breakfast, they talked about the week's experiences, and it was noted that the Noni lotion had helped Nadine's sunburn so well that they decided to make a trip back to the Macadamia nut farm and purchase a bottle to use and take home. On the way to the farm, it rained again. The rain was a refreshing memory of home.

After a quick trip into the gift shop with no chickens or chicks to be seen because of the weather, they climbed back into the car and headed back to the Airbnb to have lunch and prepare for the graduation ceremony, which was scheduled to begin at 3:00 pm. George and Martha enjoyed a chicken Caesar salad while the "kids" ate some of the leftovers from the previous few days, attempting to clear out the refrigerator in anticipation of their vacation coming to an end.

After their lunch, everyone changed their clothes to be a little more worthy of graduation. The ceremony was going to be inside, so at least they did not have to worry about umbrellas or soaking-wet seats!

George climbed into the driver's seat of the tin can while Colton took his spot as head navigator. The address for the Colosseum was punched into the GPS, and they were off. They had traveled a short distance into the city and were quickly drawn into graduation traffic, everyone having the same destination in mind. To make matters worse, the lanes of cars were being funneled from four lanes of traffic into two lines entering the parking garage.

Colton mentioned the Walmart parking lot they had attempted to park in when they first arrived in Hawaii, and everyone laughed and heaved a collective sigh of relief when they realized that they would not have such a tight turn to advance in the garage.

Parking was secured on the fourth level of the parking garage. The garage was still recovering from the rainstorms of the evening before, and the atmosphere was very humid. They walked down the stairs and followed the crowd that had formed heading for the Colosseum.

The humidity and the fact that they were all used to cooler temperatures caused everyone to break into a sweat by the time they grasped the handle of the heavy door to the Colosseum and heaved it open.

They were met with a blast of cool air from the air conditioning and felt some quick relief. Gathering together in a huddle they made a determination of what area would offer the best vantage for viewing the ceremony. The decision was made that they would sit on the side of the arena, offering a view of the graduates as they walked in. They climbed the stairs to a vacant row and settled into their chosen seats.

Everyone began to relax as they sat in the stadium seats and awaited the beginning of the ceremony. One of Luna's aunts said to

Luna that she had spotted the Rainers in the arena even before they had even caught a glimpse of Luna!

While they waited in the stands for the ceremony to start, Luna was hanging out with some of her friends. She felt strange because this was a change of life for her. She could basically do anything she wanted from this point forward.

After the group had nearly worn their eyes out from searching, Luna was finally spotted amongst the other thousands of graduates walking up the aisle to her seat. Nadine sent Luna a text message with a photo of her, officially notifying her that she had been spotted by the family. Nadine texted Luna the general location of where she was seated so that Luna could look into the stands and wave to them.

The graduation ceremony lasted about two hours. Some of Luna's friends had said to her that they wanted to leave as soon as they got their diplomas so they would not have to wait until the end of the ceremony. Their efforts were thwarted however, when they attempted to go to the restroom, only to find the exits blocked by other people.

George, Martha, Nadine, and Colton all felt conflicted about leaving the temperature-controlled arena to venture out into the hot, humid weather for the lei ceremony that was to be held on the soccer field. They all rose from their seats and walked down to the main level of the Colosseum towards the exit. They took a deep breath of cool air and shielded their eyes as the doors were opened to reveal the bright sunshine outside. They walked along the asphalt path towards the soccer field, once again following the crowd, hoping they were going in the right direction.

As they walked onto the soccer field, they spotted Luna's family gathered together in the assigned section. The field was terribly busy with other graduates' families all gathering to celebrate.

Luna soon joined everyone at the field for the lei ceremony. The lei ceremony is a time when people present the graduates with leis made from just about anything you could think of. There were flower leis, candy leis, ribbon leis, and even some constructed out of strategically folded money!

Luna was surprised at how many people had come to celebrate with her. Current classmates, former classmates, instructors, and many of her hula sisters all gathered to congratulate her. She felt very loved and appreciated and was quickly weighed down with leis of every color of the rainbow.

During the lei ceremony, Luna's mom and aunty asked the Rainiers to join them for a celebratory dinner at Liliha Bakery at the Ala Moana shopping center.

Since Luna's dad and brother had previously made plans, and they had already left in the family car, Luna elected to ride with Colton's family in the tin can rental and help direct them to the bakery.

Once again, George slid into the driver's seat, Colton took his place as navigator, and Luna squeezed into the back seat with Martha and Nadine.

When they were on the road, Luna told the Rainiers that they had been invited to her parent's house the next day for a gathering celebrating Luna and her accomplishments.

As they wound their way through the streets of Honolulu, stopping at many red lights, they were enjoying the tropical evening weather and rolled down all the car windows. They observed many signs written in the Hawaiian language. Each sign indicated a business, such as a gas station, hotel, or restaurant. One restaurant in particular caught George's eye. He chuckled to himself, and he read its name very loudly: "Phuket Thai."

Colton looked over and said, "Really, dad? All these signs, and you choose to read that one aloud?" Everyone laughed as they continued down the street in search of the bakery.

Upon arrival at the bakery, it was discovered that it had already closed for the evening. Time for plan B.

Plan B consisted of Luna, her mom, and Aunty having a quick conversation about food options. Everyone was beginning to get hungrier the later it got. The decision to go to Spiffy's restaurant was quickly made. Everyone climbed back into their vehicles and sped down the street to the restaurant's parking lot, found a space, and walked to the building's entrance.

They entered the restaurant and quickly discovered that there were no table spaces large enough to accommodate the party. Fortunately, the server was able to remove a partition between two dining booths and they were able to join each other for dinner.

This gave everyone a chance to talk and get to know one another a little better. Everyone ordered what they thought would appease their hunger, and Luna ordered a whipped orange bang beverage and immediately requested it be placed in a to-go cup as she knew she would not be able to finish it.

After dinner, Luna decided to ride home with her mom since it was already after curfew at the Airbnb. George had become so used to the area that he almost did not need Colton's navigational abilities to find their way back. As evening turned to night, George secured the car as close to the plants as he could. They entered the house, windows were opened, doors were closed and locked, and everyone went to sleep feeling pleased with how the day turned out.

# Sunday

Sunday was Mother's Day. It was always a Rainier family tradition to see who could make Mom cry with a card, a gift, or both. This year, Colton won the honor of starting the waterworks.

After a Mother's Day breakfast of fresh Hawaiian fruit, eggs, and sausage, Luna picked everyone up in her vehicle. Luna drove, Colton rode shotgun, George and Nadine shared the bench seat, and Martha squeezed and wiggled her way into the back seat with the laundry basket filled with clothes that needed washing. Luna's mom had said that Martha could save some quarters and do a load of laundry while they visited.

They went to the Aloha stadium parking lot to shop at the swap meet that took place every Sunday. Everyone looked for treasures to help remind them of their vacation. George and Martha found some t-shirts in very loud colors of orange and pink that they could wear home while Colton, Luna, and Nadine did some shopping of their own, opting for a hat for Nadine and a lot of Croc charms.

After satisfying their shopping needs, they all climbed back into Luna's vehicle and began their journey to Luna's graduation/going away party. She planned to relocate to Ohio with Colton to begin their life together, and this would be a chance for family and friends to say Aloha (goodbye).

A quick trip was made to the post office in Honolulu to mail some postcards to Missy. The post office, ironically, is located within the airport area.

As they descended off the freeway, Luna said, "Ok, here we are at the airport, bye!" Making everyone laugh at her off-handed remark.

Luna had been requested to pick up chicken katsu from Grace's Inn and malasadas (a donut-like pastry without the hole, covered in sugar) for the party at her house. As they were driving to the shopping area where they would procure these treats, George, who was sitting next to Nadine, asked, "Do you smell that?"

Nadine sniffed the air and said, "Yes, who is it?" Someone's deodorant had worn off at the swap meet. George wondered if the odor could be coming from him since he and Nadine were the only ones who could smell it. He took the chance to sniff his own armpit, nearly gagged, reminding everyone of the cat at the Dole plantation, and determined that he needed to freshen up as soon as possible.

Once they had stopped at the shopping mall, Martha, Colton and Luna went to order the malasadas from the food truck. George and Nadine went to the neighboring Starbucks to get coffee. Taking advantage of the supermarket next door, George went in and purchased new deodorant. He quickly peeled off the label and immediately applied it to his underarms. Crisis averted!

Armed with fresh armpits, coffee, chicken katsu, and warm malasadas, they were off to Luna's house for a day of relaxation and fun.

Arriving at Luna's house, everyone squirmed their way out of the vehicle and was greeted by Spot, the family dog. She was such a sweet girl and greeted everyone excitedly, wanting to be everyone's best friend.

Luna's parents and Aunties had prepared delicious food to eat, which included sushi, chicken long rice, chocolate-covered strawberries and blueberry mochi. Luna's dad lit the grill and grilled some delicious steak for everyone to enjoy.

Time passed while Luna's mom offered Martha the use of the washer and dryer to do a load of laundry. Everyone watched volleyball on television, told stories, and got to know each other better. George was enjoying watching one of the volleyball games while Luna's dad explained that the team playing was undefeated this year. Luna's brother came in and saw that they were watching the game and commented, "This team had not been defeated until this game."

Luna's dad said, "Thank you, son."

George then realized that this game had been played the day before and that this was a replay. Luna's brother had spoiled the end of the game!

They then moved to the backyard and played yard games such as bucket pong, using 5-gallon buckets filled with water and a volleyball, and Portuguese horseshoes (a game similar to cornhole played with giant washers instead of bean bags). Nadine was playing horseshoes and threw one of the washers so hard that it bounced off the plywood platform and hit a piece of scaffolding with a loud twang, making everyone stop what they were doing and look in her direction. Once it was determined that everyone was ok, laughter ensued, chatter resumed, and the games continued.

George asked Luna if he could see their pet chicken. They previously had two, but one had passed away. George always loved helping take care of their neighbors' chickens and welcomed the opportunity to pick this one up and pet it. He also found an egg! Later in the day, Nadine asked if she could see the chicken. She was petting its head and talking with it when the chicken decided to relieve itself on her arm. She refrained from throwing the chicken in disgust, set her down nicely, and quickly disappeared into the house to clean her arm.

Meanwhile, Luna was entertaining family and friends. As she walked through the kitchen, she stepped on something that squished between her toes. Luna's aunt's dog had become so excited that he had an accident. Luna quickly joined Nadine to clean up and return to the party.

Many people came and went to the party and much food was consumed. It was extremely late when Luna returned Colton's family to the Airbnb. Once again, doors were secured, windows were opened, and fans were turned on. Everyone slept very well, exhausted from a wonderful day of making memories and making new friends.

# **Monday**

Monday, the Rainier family had no plans for the day and got to sleep in. Luna was busy with packing and last-minute visits with friends and neighbors,

George, Martha, and the "kids" decided to start packing in order to ensure they had room for last-minute purchases. They watched some movies and did some last-minute shopping for souvenirs and thank-you gifts for housesitters and relatives who had assisted in getting Colton to the airport.

They climbed into the tin can and headed to the mall. George had a friend who had requested a specific type of Hawaiian candy. Colton wanted to get some Hawaii Cookie company treats for his aunt and uncle back home. Nadine said since they were going to purchase cookies, she would get some for her coworkers as an apology for missing time from work.

They arrived at the mall, found an adequate parking place, and hit the ground running. There were so many shops in the mall that there was no way they would be able to hit them all.

They looked at Crocs but decided not to purchase any. They searched several stores for the elusive requested Hawaiian candy, but it was never found. They finally found the Hawaii cookie store in the mall, where Colton and Nadine were able to purchase their gifts. George and Martha got some coffee, and they all enjoyed the natural air conditioning and tropical scents that flowed through the mall.

After walking their feet off, they returned to the parking lot and located the rental car. They navigated their way through red lights, road construction, and people to wind their way back up the hill to the Airbnb, once again bypassing the now "famous" Thai restaurant.

George carefully backed the car into its assigned parking area against the green shrubs and everyone went into the house and opened all the windows and turned on the fans.

Martha prepared lunch from the multiple leftovers in the refrigerator. With their bellies full and bodies still not used to the time differences, Colton took a nap, and Nadine decided to take a shower. George helped Martha clean the dishes and restocked the refrigerator with bottled water and cold coffee before beginning to do some packing of their own.

Meanwhile, Luna was busy at home, playing with the neighbor's dog, visiting family and neighbors, and packing what she felt would be the necessities for her relocation to Ohio.

It was not until the sun started to set and the white walls of the Airbnb turned a golden color because of the setting sun that Luna returned to the Airbnb to see Colton.

They all had dinner together as dusk turned to darkness. They gathered in the living room after dinner, each stretching out as comfortably as they could and watched another movie because, what else do you do in Hawaii when the weather is being uncooperative, and the sun has already set?

The curfew came, and Luna said her goodbyes for the evening. The doors were secured to avoid any unwelcome cockroach action, and everyone slept well that night.

# Tuesday

Tuesday would be their last full day together in Hawaii. It was spent doing more laundry, cleaning the Airbnb, and preparing for all of their trips home.

Earlier in the morning, George's telephone rang. It was the landlord asking what time they were leaving, and George said "We leave tomorrow."

The landlord answered, "You leave today, Wednesday; I have it on my calendar."

George answered, "Yes, Wednesday is tomorrow."

The landlord laughed and said, "Oh, you are correct. I guess I looked at my calendar wrong. Thank you, Aloha!"

George clicked his phone off, looked at Martha, and said, "You're not going to believe this."

As he recalled the short conversation with the landlord, Martha shook her head and said, "At least they didn't double-book us!" She looked at her phone as she silenced the alarm that was sounding and said, "Need to switch the laundry, be right back."

As Martha went out the back door, down the flight of stairs to the laundry facilities for what felt like the umpteenth time, George heard a strange sound. He went out the front door and looked up, spotting two helicopters hovering over the house. He wondered if they could be the same helicopters they had seen over the beach on Wednesday. They continued to hover for about 5 minutes. As he watched to see what their next movement might be, George had the Pink Floyd song

"Another Brick in the Wall" going through his mind: *"You, yes, you! Stand still, Laddie!"*

"Probably waiting to see if we are going to leave anytime soon," George said with a chuckle. He then waved at the cameras watching him and went back inside.

A notification sounded on George's phone. A friend who used to work with Colton had messaged him. The friend now lived in Hawaii, not too far from where they were staying, and wanted to know how long they would be there and if they all could meet up for dinner. George and Martha talked about it and thought, why not? It had been a few years since they had seen this friend, and it would be nice to catch up. George replied to his message asking where and when would be a suitable time to meet, but his messages went unread.

Luna came to the Airbnb that afternoon. They all decided that they would go down to Waikiki, watch the sunset, and then get dinner at a little pizza place called Pie-ology. Luna said that Pie-ology was well known around the island for their tasty pizza.

As the sun began to sink lower in the sky, they loaded into the rental car and started down the hill towards the touristy part of town near the beach. Parking turned out to be a minor issue as this was a popular place for watching the sunset. George did a U-turn, and they parked across the street from a reasonably populated beach.

They crossed the street, and all took their footwear off so that they could walk in the warm brown sand. They observed people parasailing, swimming, snorkeling, and playing volleyball on the beach. Many pictures were taken, and after the sun had finally sunk below the waterline of the Pacific Ocean, they climbed back into the car and went to find Pie-ology.

George checked his phone one last time to see if the friend had ever received the message about where they would be dining, but the message was still unopened.

They drove through the streets of Waikiki and entered a covered parking area. Hearing no complaints of how close the walls were or how tight the parking was, George found a parking spot, secured the car, checked for any no parking signs, and walked down three flights of stairs to a door that exited onto the sidewalk.

Once out of the garage, they were met with all sorts of sights and sounds of Hawaiian nightlife. Music, strobe lights, street vendors, and the smell of various foods being prepared made them all salivate with anticipation of having dinner. Nadine noticed a sign that said, "Gentlemen's Lounge," and asked Colton if he wanted to pay the lounge a quick visit before dinner. This comment made everyone laugh, and they suggested that they eat first and see how they felt after dinner.

They found Pie-ology, opened the glass door, and were immediately hit with the delicious smells of pizza sauce, sausage, pepperoni, melted mozzarella cheese, and rising pizza dough. They filed in and placed their orders. Martha had selected a gluten-free pizza crust that turned out to be one of the best gluten-free pizzas she had ever eaten. They pushed two tables together and everyone joined for a wonderful meal of pizza, pasta, and sodas.

After dinner, the group walked back to the parking garage. As they passed the "Gentlemen's Lounge," Nadine shoved Colton's shoulder jokingly and said, "Are you ready?"

Colton said that he had lost interest in the idea, which pleased Luna, and they continued to the car. Everyone took their assigned seats in the car, and they made a quick cruise through Waikiki. Windows down and music up. They enjoyed a few minutes of tropical air before making their ascent up the hill and returning to the Airbnb. Luna said her goodbyes for the evening, and they made a plan to get together at the airport the next day. George, Martha, and Nadine would fly home earlier in the day, and Colton would return to Luna's house to gather her belongings and begin their journey later in the day.

One last nightly routine of checking windows and doors for unwanted visitors was made, and everyone retired for the night.

# Wednesday

Time to go home.

Everyone slept in that last day as much as they could. For the most part, they had enjoyed their getaway, but they were all yearning for normalization and sleeping in their own beds.

After a quick breakfast consisting of the last of the fresh fruit and breakfast sandwiches, a quick clean of the Airbnb was completed. It consisted of stripping sheets from the beds, piling towels on the tile floor of the bathroom, placing decorative plants back in their places, moving fans back into the hallway, and closing the windows. Every floor was swept to ensure not a grain of sand was left behind. With the last of the packing completed, a game of car luggage Tetris was once again played in preparation for the drive to the airport.

It was a bright, sunny morning. A perfect Hawaiian day after all the intrepid weather they had encountered over the last week.

They spent a few minutes talking with the little green geckos on the front porch. The small reptiles had begun to change color to match the brown stain of the porch railings and bore a streaked pattern of brown and green. The geckos were not nearly as enthusiastic as the people to be spending time together and quickly scurried into a gap between the porch deck and skirting.

George and Martha made one last scan of the house and property, ensuring that none of their personal belongings had been left behind and that they had hung the decorative broom back on the wall. They placed the garbage and recycling in the appropriate containers and made their way to the car.

Nadine and Colton were standing in the bright Hawaiian sunshine waiting for George to move the car so that they could open the doors that were currently inaccessible because of being parked so close to the plants and railing.

George set the combination code on the door lock for the last time, looked at the camera, and waved. He then strode up the stairs, climbed in the car, and moved it enough to allow everyone else to get in their assigned seats. As everyone buckled up, George's phone chimed one more time indicating that the Wi-Fi from the Airbnb had been turned off and their devices had been disconnected.

The return trip to the airport was non-eventful. They overpaid for gas to fill the car and pulled into the same underground parking area, turning in the car. The attendant scanned the code on the dashboard, and everyone retrieved their belongings from the trunk. A double check of the cubby holes in the car was completed to make sure nothing was left behind except the sand from the beach that had fallen off the ice chest days before.

They made their way to the Hawaiian Airlines gate, and George, Martha, and Nadine checked in for their short flight to Maui, a small layover, and then the trip back to Seattle.

While they were checking in, Luna was circling her way through the airport parking structure, having difficulties determining which way to go. She finally found a parking spot at the very top of the structure. She secured her vehicle, making sure it was parked legally and went to the elevators. She called Colton in an attempt to locate where they were.

Luna finally caught up with Colton and the family in a very crowded airport as they were saying their goodbyes. Nadine hugged

Luna and asked if she could find a map of Oahu before they left later that day and mail it to her. George and Martha had tearful goodbyes as they parted ways with Colton.

Colton and Luna watched George, Martha, and Nadine until they disappeared into the TSA line. They then turned and began walking to the parking garage.

Luna and Colton were walking through the garage, looking for her car, when Luna told him that she was not sure that she remembered where she had parked. She said that because the airport was so confusing, she could only recall that she had parked on the top of the structure. Everything seemed like a maze, but eventually, they found her vehicle and drove to Luna's parents' house to gather her belongings and say a few last-minute goodbyes while preparing for their trip to Ohio.

George, Martha, and Nadine found their departure gate and three seats they could occupy until boarding. There were hula performers in the waiting area of the terminal, and they enjoyed listening to Hawaiian music and watching the dancers. Many small birds soared through the terminal and landed near them, hopping closer in hopes of snatching a stray crumb that might have fallen on the ground.

Once on board the plane, George was sitting a few rows ahead of Martha and Nadine. As the plane approached the runway it suddenly banked to turn the corner and quickly sped up. It felt as if the front tire of the plane struck a pothole in the runway, making it feel as if the plane had somehow popped a wheelie. Martha and Nadine started laughing and began leaning forward as if attempting to help the plane get the wheel back on the ground.

Nadine feared she may experience some air sickness when the plane had taken off, recalling the last flight to Maui. Martha encouraged her to focus on the exit sign in front of them. Martha looked out and saw the pretty blue color of the ocean and told Nadine to look. Suddenly, she remembered that Nadine was not feeling well and said, "No! Focus on the sign!" causing them both to laugh even harder.

The approach and landing in Maui reminded them of a roller coaster and the feeling you get when you suddenly lurch down the track. Only this ride was repetitive in that feeling as they dropped lower and lower to the ground. The plane's landing gear was lowered with a loud grinding noise and an even louder thunk. The pilot eased onto the runway and immediately deployed the brakes because of the short runway. Once they were safely on the ground, George looked back at the girls and mouthed, "What the F*** was that?" causing them all to laugh, thankful to be safely on the ground.

After a short bathroom break, they decided they needed some food. Their departure gate had been changed, and their flight was delayed, so they went to the restaurant and ordered burgers, fries, and some sodas to help settle their stomachs. The food was worth the wait, and the burgers were some of the best they had had in quite some time.

The time for boarding their final flight finally came. George, Martha, and Nadine heaved a collective sigh of relief when they discovered they could finally sit together for the last longer stretch of their trip.

While the Washington-bound trio was making their way home, Luna and Colton were still in Hawaii preparing for their trip, which would not even begin until the others had landed in Seattle.

The flight from Maui to Seattle was long. Sleep was not an option for them because of the constant chatter and the continuous crying of children.

Finally landing in Seattle, George, Martha, and Nadine pulled their jackets out of their carry-on bags and prepared to exit the aircraft. They looked over their shoulders, and all agreed they would not miss the crying toddler two rows back.

After claiming their luggage, they headed across the sky bridge to the parking lot, where they would meet the shuttle bus to take them to their car. Suddenly, they heard a familiar screech of a toddler; the same child who sleep had evaded on the flight was still crying. Crossing the sky bridge back towards the airport, he was using a wheeled suitcase as a makeshift walker while his mother followed, trying to get him to stop screaming and return to their vehicle. George was amazed that the child was still awake and haunting them until the end of their trip!

The three of them packed into the hotel courtesy shuttle and were whisked back to the parking lot where they had left their vehicle.

George tipped the driver as they transferred their luggage into their own vehicle. After a week of driving the rental car, George nominated Martha to drive the two-and-a-half hours to their home. There was no need for them to play rock, paper, scissors.

George, Martha, and Nadine walked into their home, greeted the family cat, quickly changed into pajamas, brushed their teeth, and fell exhausted into bed.

Luna and Colton were traveling back to Luna's house but had to make several stops on the way. They went to the local 7-11 store to pick up travel snacks since they would have such a long layover in Phoenix.

When they finally arrived at the house, Spot saw Colton and went crazy. Barking, circling, lunging towards and shying away from him, trying to decide if he was a friend or foe. Colton stayed where he was, said hi to Spot, and waited for her to calm down. After a brief time, Spot decided that he was a friend, calmed down, and laid with them in the living room.

Luna was trying to decide what she wanted to have for lunch since this would be her last day on the island for a while. She finally decided they should get lumpia and dippin' dots. Luna drove Colton to the Waikele shopping center. While they were driving through the parking lot, they saw a store called LAX. Not knowing what it was, they decided to check the store out after they purchased their dippin' dots. They found out that LAX was actually a barber shop. Colton had no need for a haircut, so they were quickly on their way to the next store. They were shopping for Croc charms when Luna's phone rang. It was her family saying she needed to pick up the lumpia and bring it to the house because her brother would be leaving soon, and she did not want to miss saying goodbye to him.

When they returned to the house, Spot was again confused about Colton. Luna was relaxing and decided to feed Spot some carrots. Suddenly, she had an idea. She asked Colton to feed Spot carrots so that she might stop barking and lunging at him and calm down. The carrots did the trick, and once again, Spot lay at the feet of her new friend.

With time to kill, Luna decided to show Colton a new video game called "Around The Island." It was a series of mini games which gave them clues to follow to travel around the island. Luna thought she would win the game because she had lived on the island her entire life, but Colton wound up winning.

A little while later, Luna's family decided to take Colton and her to Gykaku for dinner. Other relatives joined them, and they had a wonderful time catching up and saying their last-minute goodbyes.

After dinner, they were driving back to the house and Luna heard a clang come from somewhere under the vehicle. Her dad kidded her and said, "You broke the van."

Luna said, "I didn't even drive the van today. YOU broke it!" They laughed and decided they would use a different vehicle to go to the airport later that day.

Since Luna's dad did not eat at the restaurant, he decided to grill some food at home. He was joking around with the tongs, and Luna laughed and said he looked like a crab.

They laughed about the events of the day on their drive to the airport. Luna's family accompanied them to the ticketing counter, and their laughter changed to sadness as they said their tearful goodbyes at the TSA line.

Luna is a short person, so Colton, being the gentleman that he is, volunteered to carry her carry-on baggage through the airport and onto the plane. Colton could feel the other passengers giving him the evil eye because he was carrying more than the two-bag per passenger limit.

They both tried to sleep on the plane, but the lady seated next to Luna had a tablet that she was using, and the screen brightness was so high that it looked like the overhead light was on.

It was morning by the time they landed in Phoenix. They ate the spam musubi and manapua that they had purchased before leaving Hawaii for lunch. They slept in shifts, one of them awake enough to watch their belongings. Luna slept on a row of chairs, but Colton, being a tall person, actually wound up sleeping on the floor of the airport using one of their carry-ons as a pillow while they waited for their next flight.

It was hot in Arizona and inside the airport as they were having problems with the HVAC system. They plodded their way to their departure gate and waited while they watched several flights land and take off from that gate, wishing each time that it was their flight.

They watched a plane land and unload at the gate, but their flight was not allowed to begin boarding. Suddenly, an announcement came over the speakers saying that the plane was waiting for a part so repairs could be made to it, causing their flight to be delayed once again. Colton began having flashbacks of the movie "The Terminal" as he planned on what bathroom he would need to use to freshen up while they lived in the airport waiting for their turn to leave.

While Colton and Luna paced the terminal anxiously awaiting their flight, Luna paused to look out the window and saw someone's legs hanging out of an aircraft. She watched as the legs wiggled back and forth and hoped that this person was someone working on the aircraft and not a stowaway that had flown in from who knew where!

A few hours later, they realized their flight would depart from a different gate. They gathered their belongings and sprinted to the gate. They were able to make it on the plane just in time.

A couple of hours into the flight, they watched the sunset from inside the airplane. Soon, they saw city lights and realized they were close to landing at their destination.

The airport was nearly abandoned when they finally landed, and it looked like it was closed. They quickly secured their luggage and waited for their ride. Luna finally got to meet more of Colton's relatives when they were picked up from the airport.

They spent the night with his relatives, and after a wonderful breakfast, they made their way to Colton's apartment to begin new chapters in both of their lives. New experiences lay ahead for Luna and Colton, but first… More Sleep…